THE BOXCAR CHILDREN®

CREATED BY
GERTRUDE CHANDLER WARNER

ENDANGERED ANIMALS

BOOK 2

Mystery of the Spotted Leopard

ALBERT WHITMAN & COMPANY
CHICAGO, ILLINOIS

ISBN 978-0-8075-1019-3 (hardcover)
ISBN 978-0-8075-1020-9 (paperback)
ISBN 978-0-8075-1021-6 (ebook)

Printed in the United States of America
10 9 8 7 6 5 4 3 2 1 LB 26 25 24 23 22

Illustrations by Craig Orback

Visit The Boxcar Children® online at www.boxcarchildren.com.
For more information about Albert Whitman & Company,
visit our website at www.albertwhitman.com.

CONTENTS

The Boxcar Children are helping endangered animals!

The group spread out, with Henry on one end and their guide, Kayla, on the other. Everyone scanned the ground as they moved through the tall grass.

Violet was the first to spot something. She called out and held up a plastic water bottle.

"I guess we're not the first people to come this way," Jessie said.

They kept going, and before long, Jessie gave a shout.

"More garbage?" Violet asked.

Jessie crouched in the tall grass. "I don't think so."

The group gathered around, and Jessie handed the thing to Kayla.

"It's the GPS collar," Kayla said. "This didn't come off by accident. Someone removed it."

Benny gulped. "But if the collar is here, where is the snow leopard it belongs to?"

CHAPTER 1

A New Adventure

"I can't wait to see the real thing," said ten-year-old Violet Alden, adding spots to the drawing in her sketch pad. "I'll draw an even better one then."

"I'd say your snow leopards look pretty good already," Henry said from across the airplane aisle. Then he turned back to the book about India he was reading to his little brother, Benny.

At fourteen, Henry was the oldest of the four Alden children. He was used to watching out for the others. On this trip, he had a lot of responsibility. The children were on a flight halfway around the world. Until they landed, he was in charge. And with six-year-old Benny, that meant making sure he didn't get too antsy.

Jessie reviewed the notes she'd written in her notebook. She was twelve and liked to keep the children's travels organized. "We will land in Leh," she said. "That is the largest city in Ladakh."

"Huh?" said Benny. "I thought we were going to India."

"Ladakh is a territory in India," Jessie explained. "It's in the northern part of the country. It's also one of the highest up places in the world."

Henry nodded. "A perfect place for snow leopards," he said. "They live far up in the mountains. And the Himalayas have the highest peaks anywhere."

A voice came over the airplane's speakers announcing that they would be landing soon. Violet closed her sketch pad. Jessie tucked her notebook into her backpack. Henry put away the book he was reading and made sure everyone had their seat belts on.

Benny bounced in his seat. "I can't wait to see Kayla again!"

Kayla Young was the family friend the Aldens planned to meet at the airport. She worked for a group called Protectors of Animals Worldwide, or PAW. The children had met Kayla when they were visiting Port Elizabeth, where she'd been doing research. After a bad oil spill had happened off the coast, they'd helped her keep the animals that were affected safe. Kayla had been so impressed with their help, she'd invited them to come along as she helped protect other animals around the world.

Benny gazed out the window as the plane descended. They'd been flying above clouds. Now mountain ranges stretched as far as he could see. The tops of the mountains were white with snow.

"Everything is so big," said Benny. "It must be hard to find snow leopards in the mountains."

Violet leaned over to look. "I bet they can go all kinds of places people can't. They probably hide well too."

"That's why Kayla and PAW need to study them," Jessie said. "PAW wants to find out how snow leopards act in the wild. They also want to know how people are affecting the cats."

Benny looked up at his big sister. "What do you mean? I like to pet cats and hear them purr."

Jessie grinned. "Don't try to pet a snow leopard. They're wild animals."

"I know," Benny said. "We shouldn't touch wild animals. We might hurt them, or they might hurt us."

"Right," said Henry. "I don't think you'll have a chance to touch a snow leopard anyway. They won't want to get close to us. But maybe we'll see one, if we're lucky."

Violet sighed. "I sure hope so. It would be sad to come all this way and never see a snow leopard."

"It will still be fun," Benny said. "We get to be in the mountains. Grandfather said it's really far from

4

everything. It will be like living in the boxcar again."

At one time, the children had lived in a boxcar in the forest. That was after their parents had died. They'd thought their grandfather would be mean, so they'd run away. They'd had many adventures while living in the boxcar, but when Grandfather had found them, they'd found out he wasn't mean at all. Now they had a real home with Grandfather, and they still had plenty of adventures.

Jessie chuckled. "Benny, the Himalayan wilderness might be a little tougher than the forests of Greenfield, Connecticut."

They watched as the plane lowered into a wide valley. A blue-gray river wound between green trees. Buildings came into view.

Before long, the plane touched down. Benny giggled as the plane bounced on the runway and slowed to a stop. When the plane reached the gate, a flight attendant escorted the children off the plane.

Finally, after hours of travel, the Aldens saw a friendly face. Kayla had big, smiling brown eyes, and her short hair bounced as she hurried over to greet them with hugs. She'd already been in India for a week and had traveled down from the PAW research center in the mountains to pick up the children.

Once everyone was ready, the Aldens followed Kayla outside, where a shuttle was waiting to pick them up. Benny yawned. "What time is it? It's bright out, but I feel like it's the middle of the night."

"We traveled a long time," Henry said. "Back home, it would be the middle of the night."

"You're also at a very high altitude," Kayla said. "Here we're more than eleven thousand feet up. The tallest mountain in New England isn't much higher than six thousand feet."

Jessie looked at the mountains rising in the distance. "And we aren't even to our final destination yet."

"No," said Kayla, "but the air is thinner at this height. It has less oxygen in it, which makes it harder to breathe. We'll rest here in Leh to get used to the altitude. Then we'll go to the research center farther up."

Violet took a deep breath. "Does that mean even less air?" she asked.

Kayla put an arm around Violet's shoulders. "It does. But don't worry, we'll take it slow. Plus, you kids are in good shape. I saw the way you ran around the beach back in Port Elizabeth."

After a short shuttle ride, the Aldens reached the hotel and took their bags to their rooms. Once they were settled in, they could really feel the effects of the long flight. The children climbed into comfy beds, and one by one, they fell asleep. A new adventure was about to begin, and they needed to be rested for it.

❖

"I'm feeling better now," Violet said that evening as the children headed to meet Kayla for dinner in the hotel dining room.

The others agreed, even Benny. "Usually, I don't like to nap because I don't want to miss anything," he said. "Today I knew everyone would be napping!"

At dinner, Kayla filled in the Aldens about the research PAW was doing in India. "Snow leopards are elusive," she said. "That means they are hard to find. Here, some people call them the 'ghosts of the Himalayas.'"

"Ghosts!" Benny laughed. "Not real ghosts though."

Henry nudged his brother. "There aren't any real ghosts, silly."

"Maybe there are," Benny said. "We haven't seen any, but we haven't seen any snow leopards yet either."

Kayla chuckled. "In this case, 'ghosts of the Himalayas' just means that snow leopards are very hard to spot."

"Don't leopards already have spots?" Benny giggled at his own joke.

"Actually, they don't really have spots," Jessie said. "They have rough black circles shaped kind of like roses. They're called rosettes." Jessie had been learning all about snow leopards in the days leading up to their trip.

"Very good," said Kayla, looking impressed. "Other leopards have golden fur with black rosettes. Snow leopards have light gray fur with black rosettes." She smiled at Benny. "Or spots."

"How many snow leopards are left?" Violet asked.

"We think there are fewer than eight thousand," Kayla said.

"In the whole world?" said Benny.

"That's right," said Kayla. "But it's difficult to get a good count. They live in steep, snowy mountains, and few roads go through their territory. Mostly that's good. It keeps away people who might hurt them. But it's bad for researchers like me who want to find them. Even people working here for many years might never see a wild snow leopard."

As Jessie finished eating, she pulled out her notebook to make notes. "How do you study an animal you can't see?"

"We get help from technology," Kayla said. "First we look for places we think the snow leopards go. We look for tracks or other signs of the animal's presence. Then we can put up cameras that record if a cat passes by."

Jessie scribbled notes. "Can you tell much from the pictures?"

"Not as much as we'd like," said Kayla. "Sometimes we capture an animal. Then we can examine it to make sure it's healthy. We also put a collar on it with a special GPS unit. Then we release the animal, and the GPS sends a signal to our computers so we can see where it goes. The leopard gets to live its life in the mountains, and we learn where it travels."

"That's really cool," Jessie said.

"I was hoping to see a snow leopard." Violet frowned. "A photo isn't the same."

"You've come at the right time," said Kayla. "At the research station, we've been tracking a female snow leopard through its GPS collar. We're learning a lot about her range, or the area she travels. It's important work to help protect the species."

"If we know where it is, maybe we can spot it!" Benny said.

Kayla nodded. "We just might," she said. "But I don't want you to be disappointed if we don't get the chance. Sometimes the best place for a wild animal is in the wild. Usually, if a snow leopard comes near humans, it means something is wrong. When they are away from humans, they are safest and happiest."

Violet thought of her drawing of a snow leopard. She really did want to see a snow leopard in person. But more than anything, she wanted to do what she could to make sure the animal would be safe and happy.

She hoped they could find a way to do both.

CHAPTER 2

A Change of Plans

The next morning, the Aldens woke up excited to explore. They headed down to the hotel restaurant for breakfast. The buffet had some familiar foods, like scrambled eggs and roasted vegetables. Benny especially liked the warm buns with apricot jam.

Henry tried a warm drink that wasn't so familiar.

"Butter tea is traditional here," said Kayla. "This

is a special kind called *pu-erh*. Personally, I think it tastes like soil, but it's not so bad with some milk, yak butter, and salt."

Benny wrinkled his nose. "Dirt tea with salt and yak butter? No thank you."

Henry lifted the bowl of tea and took a cautious sip. "It is different. It doesn't taste like any other tea I've tried." He sipped some more. "It's thick and sort of sour. I'm not sure if I like it. Maybe."

"Well, it's very high in calories," Kayla said. "That's good when you work outside in the cold. Butter tea for breakfast gives you lots of energy."

Henry passed the bowl around so his brother and sisters could try it. Trying new things was always fun. They decided they'd rather have juice with breakfast though.

After breakfast, the Aldens bundled up in warm clothes. Kayla led them out to the streets of Leh. The sun shone brightly in the blue sky.

Jessie put on sunglasses. "My eyes tell me it's daytime, but I'm still tired, even though I slept a long time."

Violet covered a yawn. "Me too. I feel funny. Not dizzy exactly but a little off-balance."

"That's normal when you first get to this high elevation," Kayla said. "Remember, you need to give your bodies time to get used to the thin air."

Even Benny wasn't as bouncy as usual. Normally he led the way, but now he had to work hard to keep up, even though Kayla wasn't walking quickly.

Jessie stopped to pick up a plastic water bottle someone had dropped in the street. "Ugh. I guess trash is a problem everywhere." She looked around for a garbage can but didn't see one.

Kayla took the bottle and put it in her backpack to throw away later. "It's a huge problem here. Tourists create so much trash. They dump thousands of plastic water bottles each summer."

"That's terrible," Jessie said. "I'm glad we brought water bottles we can refill."

Henry nodded. "Just remember to be careful when you refill. Remember what Grandfather told us? We need to make sure the water won't make us sick."

"That's right," Kayla said. "Leh used to get its water from melting glaciers, but most of the glaciers are gone now, sadly. The streams around here are polluted as well. Even the local people have to buy bottled water now."

"I never thought about not having clean water," Jessie said. "We take it for granted that we have all the water we want."

The children came to a wide street paved with bricks. Some of the bricks were colored orange, yellow, or white, making square and diamond designs.

"This is the main market," Kayla said.

The street was closed to cars, so people could walk from side to side without worrying about traffic. Rows of pretty buildings three stories high ran along each side. People sat on the sidewalks next to piles of vegetables for sale. The Aldens recognized potatoes, onions, carrots, and other familiar foods. They also saw others they didn't recognize.

"Look at all the food!" Benny took a deep breath of the cool air. "It smells good here. I smell bread baking and vegetables cooking and maybe soup like we had at the hotel last night."

One window showed racks of bread. Benny hurried toward it and peered inside at all kinds of bread, rolls, pastries, muffins, and cookies. His mouth watered. "Can we try some?"

Kayla laughed. "You just had breakfast. I promise we'll have a tasty lunch in a couple of hours."

Benny sighed. "That sounds like a long time. We need to keep up our energy because it's cold and the air is thin."

"You learn quickly." Kayla smiled. "But I promise you won't starve."

They walked past a shop with bunches of bananas hanging from the ceiling. Inside, they heard people talking quickly in a language that Kayla said was Ladakhi.

Violet took pictures of the shops and the street market. She loved all the bright colors. She'd need her colored pencils to draw this.

Partway down the block, someone was speaking

loudly in a language the children recognized. "Protect the snow leopards! Put them back on the endangered species list." The man was in his twenties. He had long brown hair and a sunburned nose. He wore a shirt with a picture of snow leopard on it and spoke with an American accent. The man held out pamphlets to everyone who passed.

The children stopped to listen. "I thought snow leopards were endangered," Jessie said to Kayla.

"They were recently taken off the endangered species list," the man chimed in. He handed Jessie a pamphlet. "Now they're only considered vulnerable. But that's not good enough. There are only a few thousand left!"

Violet whispered to Kayla. "I forget. What's the difference between endangered and vulnerable?"

"The categories tell how likely it is that a species will become extinct," Kayla said. "*Extinct* means we don't think there are any more individuals anywhere. Once something is extinct, it's gone forever. Some animals are extinct in the wild. That

means they survive only in captivity, like in zoos or aquariums. *Endangered* means an animal is at high risk of going extinct. *Vulnerable* isn't quite so serious. It means the species might become endangered if we don't take action."

"So vulnerable isn't as bad as endangered." Violet took a pamphlet from the man.

"Snow leopards almost went extinct," he said. "Their numbers have come back a little, but not enough."

"You said there are around eight thousand snow leopards, right?" Henry asked Kayla.

"We think between six and eight thousand," she replied. "They're so hard to find though. We need to confirm how many there are. That's one reason we're doing our studies. Even if their numbers are growing, we need to know how to protect them."

"That's right!" The man handed a pamphlet to Kayla and introduced himself. "My name is Oliver Jacobs. I'm here with a group of activists. We're trying to spread awareness about snow leopards."

Kayla flipped through the pamphlet. "Interesting. I work with an organization doing research on snow leopards."

Oliver gave pamphlets to Henry and Benny. "I'm always happy to meet other animal lovers," the man said. "It's hard to find anyone who cares as much as we do."

"If snow leopard numbers are growing, isn't that good?" Violet asked.

"Sure, but that doesn't mean it's time to remove the protections." Oliver waved his arms. "We can't wait until it's too late to make more changes."

"What kind of changes?" Jessie asked.

"Some people still kill snow leopards," Oliver said. "Some people do it because leopards have attacked their livestock, but the leopards are just trying to survive. People also hunt the leopards' natural prey, like wild sheep. That means the leopards have to kill livestock to eat."

Kayla nodded. "That makes the farmers unhappy. Losing even one goat or sheep is hard for them."

"That's no excuse," Oliver said. "My group is

trying to get the local people to leave the leopards alone. People have done so much damage to the animals. Now we have to save them."

The children were happy to hear that Oliver was so excited about helping snow leopards. But Kayla gave a sigh. "It's not quite so simple," she said. "We have to work with the local people."

"We have to do whatever it takes," Oliver said. Then he hurried toward another group of tourists, waving his pamphlets.

"He certainly is passionate," said Violet. "It's good to see people talking about the problems snow leopards are facing."

"He must have been here for a while," Jessie said. "He has lots of energy even at this altitude. I'm feeling a bit better though. What's next?"

"How about some history?" Kayla asked.

On the other side of the market, they entered a narrow alley with fewer people. Here the buildings weren't painted and didn't look as new.

"We're entering Old Town," Kayla said. "This

area only opened to tourism in 1974. I suppose that sounds long ago to you kids. It's actually quite recent. Few outsiders came here before that. Now more than two million people visit this area most years."

The group wandered through a maze of alleys. It was like stepping back in time. The buildings had low wooden doors warped from age, and tall, skinny windows with wooden shutters.

Violet touched one of the rough walls. "This looks like mud."

"Yes, the walls are made of mud bricks," Kayla said. "These buildings are centuries old."

"It's hard to believe mud can last hundreds and hundreds of years," said Violet. She took pictures so she could sketch the neighborhood later.

"A lot of this area has been destroyed," Kayla said. "Some buildings were knocked down to make room for newer buildings. Flash floods destroyed some buildings a few years back. But people are trying to protect some of these old buildings."

"Like they're trying to protect the snow leopards?" Benny asked.

Kayla hummed in thought. "We want to protect nature because it's good for the planet," she said at last. "For example, forests help make oxygen that all living things breathe. Animals that eat grass, like elephants and zebras, keep wildfires from spreading. Nature works better when we protect all of it—so every animal and plant can do its part."

"Besides, I like animals," Jessie said. "Imagine a world without elephants or polar bears or dolphins. It wouldn't be such a wonderful place."

"Absolutely," Kayla said. "As for protecting history, that helps us understand the past. It helps us respect the cultures that were here before and that are here now. It helps us learn about each other."

"I like to learn about places by trying different food," Benny said.

Kayla laughed. "That's a good way to appreciate different cultures too. Let's head back and find some lunch."

After leaving the old part of Leh, the group found a restaurant, where they ordered bowls of soup with noodles and vegetables. It was the perfect way to warm up on a chilly day.

As they were finishing up, Kayla suddenly set down her spoon and pulled out her phone. She studied the screen and frowned.

"Is everything all right?" Henry asked.

"I'm afraid not," Kayla said. "This message is from one of the other researchers. She was tracking a cat called Tashi—the one I was telling you about—through its GPS collar. Late last night, it looked like Tashi was coming toward the village where the research center is located."

"That's strange," said Henry. "You said that the leopards like to keep their distance from humans."

Kayla nodded. "That's not the strangest thing. As the GPS got closer, it suddenly stopped moving or sending a signal."

The children looked at one another. That did sound like bad news.

"I think we should get back to the hotel." Kayla pushed back her chair and stood. "I want to get to the research center and help look for Tashi."

The children rose. Benny grabbed the rest of his bread to eat as they walked.

"Do you think someone hurt her?" Violet asked.

"I don't know," said Kayla, hurrying along. "My friend says it's probably just a problem with the tracking collar. I think she's worried though. Even if Tashi is okay, we're losing important data. I was going to stay here with you for a few days so you could adjust to the altitude, but I really need to get back there."

Henry looked at his siblings. "We want to go with you."

The others nodded.

Kayla looked unsure. "It will be hard at the higher altitude," she said.

"We understand," Henry said. "But maybe we can help."

Kayla was quiet for a moment. "All right," she said finally. "You've adjusted well so far, and I can't leave you behind. I'll start making plans."

As Kayla led the way back to the hotel, the children hurried to keep up. They wanted to show they wouldn't slow down the research team.

"I hope nothing happened to Tashi," Violet said. "Every snow leopard is important."

"It doesn't sound good," said Henry. "But whatever happened, we'll help Kayla get to the bottom of it."

CHAPTER 3

Give and Take

As Kayla made plans that evening, the children rested at the hotel. They wanted to keep exploring the city of Leh, but they were tired from the altitude, and they wanted to be around to hear any updates from the research center about Tashi. No news came, but the following morning, after a tasty breakfast, the Aldens checked out and left the hotel.

Outside, Kayla introduced them to a woman standing next to a large truck with huge tires. "This is Meera Dewan," Kayla announced. "She's a tour guide who has agreed to bring us up to the research station. We're lucky to have gotten her on short notice."

Meera gave a small nod to the children before grabbing the Aldens' bags and putting them into the back of the van. "Get in," she said.

Violet paused to look at the snow leopard painted on the side of the van.

"Hurry now," Meera ordered. "We have a long drive."

Kayla whispered to the children as they climbed into the van. "Meera isn't really grumpy. She's just always thinking about what needs to be done. She'll drive us to the village today, and later she'll help us look for snow leopards. She's an excellent tour guide."

"Just one more now," Meera said from outside. "A late addition."

Jessie wondered who might be joining them on

the journey into the mountains.

She got her answer a moment later as a man with long brown hair and a sunburned nose hauled his backpack up to the van. "I'm here! Don't leave without me!" It was the man from the day before, Oliver Jacobs. He dropped his pack at the back of the van and then got into the front passenger seat. He twisted to look at the children. "Hello again. You're heading into the bush too, I see."

"Bush?" Benny asked. He had hardly seen any bushes since arriving in India. "We're going into the mountains."

Oliver laughed. "The wilderness. In Australia they call it the bush. I was there last year trying to save the wombats."

The tour guide, Meera, got in the driver's seat in time to hear that. She snorted. "So you're one of those people. You think you get to tell the locals what to do."

Oliver's eyes opened wide. "I'm only trying to save animals."

"Sure." Meera started the truck. "You are another tourist. Fine by me. Tourists bring in money." She pulled out into traffic.

"I'm no tourist," Oliver said, crossing his arms. "I'm an activist."

Kayla tried to change the subject. "What brings you to such a remote place?" she asked. "We're going because the village is the base of the leopard research program. What do you hope to do there?"

"I'm joining some friends. We need to convince people to leave the cats alone." Oliver scowled. "The snow leopards don't need to be researched. They need people to stay away and let them live in peace."

"Wait a minute," Kayla said, crossing her arms. "I thought we were on the same side. PAW is doing research to learn where the snow leopards live and travel. We want to find out what they're eating and how often they need to hunt. We can't protect them if we don't know their behavior."

"If everyone stayed away, it wouldn't be a problem." Oliver faced forward and sank into silence.

Henry and Jessie shared a look. Like the day before, the children could tell Oliver wanted to help the snow leopards. But something about the way he spoke to Kayla didn't seem right.

The truck sped through the streets of Leh, dodging the busy traffic. Soon they were on a road out of town. The children peered out the windows as the road passed between rugged hills. Mountains with snowy peaks rose in the distance. Some of the mountaintops disappeared into the clouds.

Meera spoke over the noise of the engine. "Ladakh is the Land of High Passes. Once, ancient trade routes came through here. Caravans carried many goods: cloth, spices, coffee, and tea."

"Caravans?" Jessie asked. The word made her think of a line of travelers moving through the desert. "Like people on camels?"

"Sometimes camels," said Meera. "More often yaks, donkeys, and ponies. All traveling to the market in Leh."

The road started winding through sharp turns as

it climbed higher. On one side was a steep slope that went up, and on the other, a steep slope led to a valley below, where a river curved between green fields.

"It's hard to imagine traveling through here before people had cars or paved roads," said Henry.

"People traveled without them for thousands of years," Meera said. "The traders only came in the summer though. They couldn't travel the high passes between valleys until the snow melted."

"Now you have tourists in the winter," Oliver said. "So many tourists come to see the snow leopards. People race all over the mountains pestering the poor cats."

Kayla frowned. "You talk like a leopard can't nap without someone taking its picture. Most people go home without ever seeing a snow leopard."

"That may be," Oliver said, "but fifty thousand people come to Ladakh every month. You can't have that many people without disturbing the leopards."

Jessie pulled out her notebook to make some notes on the conversation.

"Meera," said Henry, "do most people come here hoping to see the snow leopards?"

"I don't know about most tourists," Meera said. "But my biggest business is snow leopards. Many foreigners want to see them. Kayla is right though— not everyone gets to see the big cats."

Oliver glared at her. "Tours like yours are part of the problem."

"Then what am I supposed to do?" Meera waved a hand in the air before grabbing the steering wheel again. "I make my living from people who want to see snow leopards. The old way of doing things is long gone."

She laughed. "Tourism is a big business! In fact, I don't have time for all the people who want tours. When it's busy, I have to hire other guides to help. I have two trucks and five snowmobiles. If I get any more, I will need a bigger garage. Maybe I should just open a zoo and charge a fee. That way everyone could see a snow leopard, and I wouldn't pay so much for gas for my big trucks."

Jessie wrote down "zoo." Then she crossed it out. Meera had probably been joking.

"What other work do people do here?" Henry asked.

"Most people are farmers," Meera said. "They grow barley and wheat. They raise animals—sheep, goats, cows, yaks."

"Maybe everyone should go back to farming," Oliver said.

Meera snorted. "Easy for you to say. Farming is hard work, every day—with no vacation. *You* get to live in the modern world. You have running water, indoor toilets. You don't make your food—you buy it at the shop. Why can't we have those things?"

Kayla leaned forward to tap Oliver on the shoulder. "You see what I mean about things being complicated? You want to make everyone start farming, but that wouldn't solve the problem. Farms can be hard on the land. Farmers sometimes kill snow leopards that attack their livestock."

"I didn't say it was easy," Oliver grumbled. "I still

think we have to put the animals first. Wild animals should be left alone. We shouldn't hunt them. We shouldn't capture them and put them in zoos. We shouldn't even go out looking for them. How would you feel if strangers tromped through your house, watching you?"

Violet made a face. "I wouldn't like that."

"Tourists might scare a leopard away from its meal," Oliver said. "Then it could starve or not be able to feed its babies. Even your research could change their behavior."

Jessie scribbled quickly, trying to keep up. "What do you mean?" she asked. "Can research change the thing you're researching?"

"It's called the observer effect," Oliver said. "Most animals change their behavior if they're being watched. Studies show that zoo animals act differently when visitors are around. The animals are more alert and pay attention to the visitors."

Henry looked at Kayla to check her response.

"That's true," Kayla said. "People also act

differently when they know they're being studied. Say you've been told it's polite to cover your mouth when you yawn. You might not bother when you're alone, but you do it if someone is watching."

"Ha!" Oliver exclaimed. "Even the researcher agrees with me. It gets worse. Some so-called scientists *kill* animals in the name of research."

"Are you saying we shouldn't do research?" Jessie asked.

"Yes!" Oliver shouted.

"No!" Kayla said. "I mean, we *should* do research. The problems aren't a reason not to do research. It only means we need to be careful *how* we do research. We shouldn't disturb the animals any more than we have to. That's why PAW tries to study animals in their natural habitats. We let them live their lives. We try to track their movements. We observe from a distance. The information we learn *helps* the animals."

"Tourism can help them too," Meera said. "Some of the money goes to programs that protect snow leopards and their habitats."

Jessie bit her lip as she made notes.

Henry spoke up. "Aquariums and zoos can help protect species too. They help educate people about the problems animals face. Sometimes they take in injured or sick animals and get them healthy enough to release again."

Oliver waved his hand. "Zoos are just an excuse to capture animals and take people's money."

"But people need money to live," Meera responded.

"Meera is right," said Kayla. "If we want to protect local animals, we need to think about local people too. They need a way to survive. Tourist money gives people a reason to protect the animals that tourists want to see. Tourists also learn about local people, culture, and history. Everyone wins."

Jessie looked at the notes covering her notebook pages and sighed. "It is complicated."

"You all made good points," Henry said. He agreed most with Kayla, but he didn't say that in front of Meera and Oliver. "We can find ways for the researchers, tourists, and locals to work together. At least we have to try."

But as he looked from Meera to Oliver, it didn't seem like either of them was interested in listening to the other.

CHAPTER 4

A Sound in the Night

Finally, the truck pulled into the village where the Aldens would be staying. It sat on a high plateau with mountain slopes all around. The village had only a few unpaved streets with low buildings.

Meera parked the truck in front of a small lodge with walls made of stone. She started unloading bags. Oliver grabbed his and stomped away down the street.

Jessie huddled into her coat. "I didn't know it would be so cold," she said.

"We are up in the mountains," Henry teased. "We're not going to find snow leopards on the beach."

Jessie chuckled. It felt good to joke after such a tense car ride. "I know that," she said. "The animals here have fur that traps heat. Their bodies are adapted to high mountains. I just wish mine was."

"Cold can be good," Kayla said. "The best time to look for snow leopards is in winter, when snow covers the ground." She frowned. "Or at least, snow used to cover the ground in winter. In recent years, climate change has caused problems here. They get less snow now."

"That must make the leopards sad," Benny said. "I guess they're called snow leopards because they like the snow so much."

"Actually, snow leopards live in some areas that never get much snow," Kayla said. "As long as it's high and cold, they're okay. Mostly it only causes problems for researchers. If there's snow, we might see tracks. Then we can follow the tracks or put up cameras along that path. If the leopards are walking on rocks or grass, you won't see any tracks."

Violet sighed. "It doesn't sound like we're going to see any snow leopards."

Kayla patted her shoulder. "Don't give up. PAW has been studying here for a few years. My colleagues may know where to look for snow leopards." She grabbed Benny's bag. "Come on, let's get you settled into the lodge. I'll head to the research facility to find out more about this GPS collar that's not working." She waved to Meera. "We'll see you tomorrow."

The children brought their bags to their rooms and then met in the lobby. It had low padded benches and colorful rugs on the floor. They had a warm lunch of lentils, rice, and vegetables. The man who ran the lodge was very friendly. His name was Norboo. When the children were done eating, he waved them over to the window. He looked through a telescope on a stand and moved it back and forth. After a moment, he said, "You want to see some wild ibex?"

The children took turns at the scope. They were looking at a group of brown goats on a hillside across the valley. One of the goats had huge, curved horns and a short beard.

"The one with big horns is a male," Norboo said.

"That's so exciting!" Violet said. "Thanks for showing us."

"You are welcome," Norboo said. "Snow leopards hunt the ibex. Maybe you will see snow leopards too while you are here."

"We hope so," Violet said. "At least we got to see some animals."

Jessie yawned. "I'm tired again. I guess we need more time to get used to the thin air. I don't want to miss anything though."

"I agree," Henry said. "I want to know what's happening at the research center. Let's walk over there. We can go slowly."

They bundled up in their warmest clothes and stepped outside. A man sat on the steps, plucking an instrument similar to a guitar. The children listened to the music for a minute. The village was not as busy as the city of Leh. A couple of women stood in the street, talking in their language. Some local children waved to the Aldens, who waved back.

At the edge of town, a herder tended to his flock. He wore a brown tunic that hung down to his knees over a pair of pants. His brown eyes were friendly in his lined face. "Hello," he said. "Welcome."

The children thanked him and Benny petted a sheep. "Do you live here?" Henry asked.

"I live outside town, toward the mountains, a five-minute walk." He pointed down the street. "My name is Praveer." The man gave a little bow. "I hope you will enjoy the beautiful sights of my home."

"It is very beautiful," Jessie said.

"We hope to see snow leopards." Violet was usually shy with new people. The thought of snow leopards made her too excited to stay silent though.

Praveer hesitated. Finally, he said, "If that is what you wish, I hope it for you also."

"Do you see them often?" Jessie asked.

"See them? No," Praveer said. "However, they sometimes come to my farm and kill my animals."

Violet stroked the donkey's nose. "That's sad," she said.

"It makes things hard," Praveer said. "My family needs the animals we raise. They provide milk and butter. They grow wool for making yarn. We sell the extra to buy other food." He motioned to his grazing flock. "The sheep and yaks provide meat to eat and skins for our blankets. Even the yak dung can be fuel for fires."

"Your animals must be very important to you," Henry said.

"They are everything. When my herd grows, my family is happy. We rent donkeys and yaks to the guides to carry things for tourists. Losing even one sheep to the snow leopards is a big setback. It may mean we have no money for a warm coat or new shoes."

"I wish you didn't have to worry about the snow leopards," said Violet.

Praveer smiled at her. "Thank you. It was a

problem for my father and my grandfather. Now it is my problem. But don't worry about me. I am taking care of it."

Henry wondered what he meant by "taking care of it." "There must be a way for both herders and snow leopards to get what they need," he said.

"People like to blame the herders for killing snow leopards." Praveer tapped his chest. "We only want to protect ourselves and our animals."

"We don't want to blame anyone," Jessie said, thinking back to all the notes she took during their trip to the village. "We want to find answers that help everyone. People need jobs. Animals need places to live."

"Climate change matters too, right?" Henry asked. "Our friend says there's not as much snow as there used to be. That must be bad for the snow leopards."

Praveer shook his head sadly. "The snow is melting. Glaciers are melting. Soon maybe we have no more glaciers." He gave them a big smile. "But we will not talk of such things. You must enjoy our beautiful land."

"Can I take a picture of you and your flock?" Violet asked. "I want to remember everything we learn on this trip."

Praveer stood beside his sheep as she took the photo. Then the children said goodbye and headed through the village. It wasn't hard to find the PAW research center.

Inside, Kayla introduced them to an Indian woman sitting at a computer.

"This is Sonia Chopra," said Kayla. "She lives here full time and studies the snow leopards."

Sonia waved from her seat.

"Are you from India?" Jessie asked.

"I was born in America, but my family is from India," she said. Unlike many of the people they had met in India, Sonia had an American accent. "That's one reason I wanted this job. Kayla told me you are interested in the leopards. We have been trying to find out what happened to Tashi."

The children gathered around Sonia's desk and looked at the computer screen.

"The GPS collar sends a signal," she explained. "That lets us see where the leopard has been." Sonia pointed at a line on the screen. "Here you see how Tashi usually covers the same area. This spot is a gap in the cliffs. Tashi goes up and down that crevice."

"That is so cool," Henry said. "We met a man who said snow leopards sometimes kill his livestock. With the GPS collar, you'd know if that snow leopard went to his farm."

"Yes." Sonia zoomed out on the map. "Most of the farmers live down here in the valley, close to town. We can't say for sure whether *any* snow leopard visited them, but we know if Tashi went there. Sometimes people blame the snow leopards when it might have been a fox, a wolf, a bear, or even a wild dog."

"We put up cameras at some of the farms," Kayla said. "If we don't want people to blame the snow leopards, we need to know what is really killing their livestock. Of course, sometimes it is a snow leopard. At least then we know. We can help people build better corrals to keep out predators."

Sonia tapped the computer keyboard. "Let me show you what we caught on the wildlife cameras. I'll start with some of my favorite videos."

She played some short videos. The first showed a rocky cliff. At first the Aldens didn't see anything unusual. Then, suddenly, what looked like a rock moved and came to life. It was a snow leopard! The big cat jumped down from a ledge and gracefully bounded across the screen.

Another video showed snow leopard cubs. One cub curiously approached the camera and stuck its face right in the lens so all they could see was its nose. Then it batted the camera with a paw. The camera fell over, but it kept shooting while it was on its side. The Aldens watched footage of the cubs playing for several more minutes.

Violet sighed with happiness. "They are so cute!"

"Now let's look at our most recent footage of Tashi." Sonia tapped the keyboard again. "This is from a few days ago." The camera showed a large leopard walking casually down a gap in the rocks.

"Oh, she's beautiful," Violet said. "Look at that thick fur! I just want to hug her." She giggled. "Don't worry, I won't try."

"How do you know when the snow leopards are going to be there?" Jessie asked. "Do you have to watch hours and hours of footage?"

"The cameras have motion detectors in them," Kayla said. "When something moves, the camera starts recording. We review all the recordings. Sometimes it's a different animal, like a fox or some wild sheep. We make a note of those as well. It's good to know who else uses the paths."

Sonia nodded. "Once a week I hike out to the cameras and collect the recordings. I usually have a few dozen recordings from each camera. Sometimes none of them show a snow leopard. Sometimes we get lucky and have more than one."

Jessie gave a huge yawn. "I'm sorry! It's very interesting, but I'm still tired."

Kayla smiled. "Why don't you head back to the lodge and rest? I'll be going over data this afternoon.

There won't be much for you to do here."

"You're not going to look for Tashi?" Henry asked.

"We don't know where to look yet," Kayla said. "We'll try to figure out what happened and make a plan."

"All right. We'll go back and rest," Henry said. He wanted to help, but he was feeling tired himself.

Benny gave a loud sigh. "I hate rest!"

Henry laughed. "How about a snack then?"

"I like snacks," Benny said. "And I am a little tired, so maybe some rest is okay."

They walked back through town slowly, looking at the sights. Even with the sun shining, it was cool in the mountains. At the lodge, Norboo gave them some bread and yak milk. The milk was rich and tangy. Benny smacked his lips. "It's different from cow milk, but I like it."

They had a quiet afternoon. Jessie caught up on her notes. Violet sketched the scenery outside the window. Henry and Benny played some of the board games they found in the lobby. Then everyone had a nap.

Kayla returned for dinner, looking worried. "It's strange," she told the children. "The collar shows Tashi going to an area she's never been before. Then it simply stops working. I hope a hunter didn't find her and destroy the collar."

"What are you going to do?" Jessie asked.

"Tomorrow, Meera will take us to the last place the collar sent a signal," Kayla said. "We don't know what else to do. I hope you're ready to do some hiking."

The children agreed. Everyone was excited to start helping.

❖

That night, the children gathered in the boys' room. "I'm not tired now," Jessie said. "Maybe we slept too much."

"I'm worried about Tashi," Violet said. "It's going to be hard to sleep thinking about that poor snow leopard in trouble."

"Don't worry, Violet," Benny said. "The missing

leopard is a mystery. We're good with mysteries!"

Henry smiled at his younger brother. "That's the spirit, Benny. Still, now that it's time for bed, I'm not really tired. We've seen so much in the past few days. My mind is too busy to sleep."

They talked about their trip and the sights they'd seen. Jessie read out her notes about snow leopards. "Everyone has different priorities. Oliver thinks everyone should stay away from the snow leopards. Kayla and Sonia want to do research to understand the snow leopards better. The herder, Praveer, doesn't want snow leopards eating his animals. Meera wants tourists so she can get paid to guide them to see the leopards."

"There must be a way to make everyone happy." Violet frowned. "I don't know what it is though."

A shriek cut through the night. The children sat up straighter.

"What was that?" Violet whispered. "It sounded like someone screaming."

Jessie went to the window and looked out. A few people were walking past. It was dark, but Jessie thought she recognized one of them. She pushed open the window, and cold air blew in.

"Oliver?" she called out. "Is that you?"

Most of the people outside hurried away, but Oliver turned and walked toward them. "Oh, hello. This is where you're staying?"

Jessie nodded. "Did you hear that noise?"

He didn't answer for a moment. Then he said, "What did you hear?"

The other children clustered around the window. "It sounded like someone screamed!" Benny said.

Oliver gave a weak laugh. "Oh, that was me. I stubbed my toe on a rock. These streets are so uneven."

Henry looked over Benny's head. "You made that sound?"

"Yes." Oliver laughed again. "It really hurt. I'm sure it sounded funny. My scream, I mean. Well, goodbye."

With that, Oliver turned and hurried away.

Violet leaned out the window. "He isn't walking like he has a hurt foot."

The other children watched for a moment.

Then Jessie shivered, and Henry closed the window. "You're right," he told Violet. "It was only a stubbed toe though. That can hurt a lot at first, but it's pretty easy to shake it off."

Jessie hugged herself to warm up. "I wonder why those people were out at this time of night. It's cold, and there can't be much to do here after dark."

"Maybe they were looking at the stars." Henry covered a yawn. He was starting to feel tired once again. "It's getting late, and we have a big day tomorrow. We should all try to get some sleep."

Benny crawled into his bed. "I'm going to try very hard to go to sleep. You know why?" He grinned. "Because in the morning, we get to help Kayla solve a mystery!"

CHAPTER 5

Mystery Becomes Mission

The next morning, the Aldens woke up early and headed down to the lobby to meet Kayla. Together, they had a big breakfast of bread, cheese, fruit, and apricot juice. When they were finished, they met Meera outside and piled into her truck.

Meera examined a map Kayla had printed out. "We will drive as close as we can," she said. "Then you'll need to hike."

"We're ready," Henry said. Everyone felt good that morning.

As the truck left the village, Violet looked out the window. They were nearing something with bright colors. At first she thought the large triangle shape was a tent. As they got closer, she saw many pieces of cloth strung on ropes. The cloth squares were all different colors: red and green and blue and yellow and white.

"What is that?" Violet asked. "Did someone hang laundry all the way out here?"

Meera laughed. "No laundry. Those are prayer flags."

"Prayer flags promote peace and wisdom," Kayla explained. "Each color means something different. They're supposed to give off positive spiritual vibrations."

Violent frowned. "I don't know what that means."

"Think of it as putting good thoughts into the world," Kayla said. "Each flag is like a blessing. People hang them outside where the wind blows. The wind spreads the blessings so everyone benefits. People in Tibet started using prayer flags thousands of years ago. Now they are used by Buddhists in many countries."

Meera pointed into the distance. "See those white buildings? That is a Buddhist monastery. Most people in India follow the Hindu religion. There are also many Muslims. This part of the country has more Buddhists. People come from all over to visit the monasteries."

After they passed the monastery, Meera turned onto a rough road, and the truck bumped along through the valley. Low stone walls snaked through fields of green grasses with small yellow flowers. The brown mountains rose steeply on either side. High above, craggy peaks blended with the clouds.

After a while, Meera stopped the truck. "We're close now."

Everyone got out and looked around. On Sonia's computer screen, the place had seemed close to the village. But there were no buildings for miles around.

Kayla checked her GPS.

Meera scanned the mountainsides. "Look there! Blue sheep."

The children looked where she pointed. "I don't see anything blue," Benny said.

"No, no. They are called blue sheep, but they are brown." Meera crouched beside Benny and pointed. "See? Halfway up the slope."

"Oh, I see them." Violet took a picture. The sheep were far away, but maybe they would show up in the photo. She zoomed in on the picture to check. "They have smaller horns than the sheep we saw yesterday. Why are they called blue sheep?"

"They can be a gray that is almost like blue." Meera grinned. "Also, they are not sheep. They are closer to goats."

Jessie pulled out her notebook and made a note. "I like when animals have names that describe them. It's easier to remember. This time I'll remember that they are called blue sheep because they are *not* blue or sheep. Thank you for showing us."

"Are we in the right place?" Henry asked Kayla.

"The GPS collar went past here," Kayla said. "First we'll go up to the camera traps. I told Sonia I'd collect the memory cards since we're here. Then we'll follow the GPS track as closely as we can."

They headed uphill. The rocky ground was steep, and the children had to stop often to catch their breaths. Meera marched ahead like she didn't even notice the thin air and steep slope. Every few minutes, she waited for the rest of the group.

"It doesn't look like such a hard hike," Jessie said. "I just need more air!"

"I need a snack," Benny said. "That might give me energy."

Kayla chuckled. "We'll have a snack when we get to the trail camera. It can be your reward."

Finally, the group got to the crevice in the rocky cliff. The crevice was steep enough that it would be hard for a person to climb. A few patches of snow remained in the deepest shadows.

"This is where the snow leopards like to go up and down." Kayla crouched. "You can tell one was here. That's leopard scat, or poop. And there's a paw print." She pointed at the large cat's paw print in some dried mud. A few wisps of hair clung to the rock near it. "That's snow leopard fur."

Violet took photos. If she didn't see an actual snow leopard, at least she'd seen where one had been.

Kayla passed out granola bars. "Take a break while I get the memory cards from the cameras and put in new ones."

They finished their snack and put all the wrappers in a bag so they wouldn't blow away. Violet took some pictures of the scenery. "Look at that big bird flying over the valley." It had a pale head and dark wings that stretched several feet wide.

"Himalayan vulture," Meera said. "You are lucky to see one. They're not common."

"Vultures are scavengers, right?" Henry asked. "They don't hunt like most big birds."

Meera nodded. "They look for carrion—animals killed by something else. They can eat meat several days old."

Violet wrung her hands. Seeing the vulture made her nervous for Tashi.

Kayla returned to the group holding the memory cards for the cameras. "Let's head down and follow the trail that Tashi's GPS left behind."

Going down the slope was easier than going up. Still, they went slowly because Kayla kept pausing to check the GPS. The children looked for any sign of Tashi or another snow leopard. They didn't see anything. The tall grass would hide paw prints, scats, and other signs.

"There are so many places a big cat could be hiding," Jessie said. "I wonder if we'd see one even if it was looking right at us."

"Probably not," Henry said. "Remember that video Sonia showed us?"

Jessie nodded. "We didn't see the snow leopard until it pounced down from the ledge."

Benny took Jessie's hand. He had been excited to search for the ghosts of the Himalayas, but now that they were in the wilderness, it was a little spooky.

The group came to the valley floor.

"Let's spread out," Kayla said. "The GPS says Tashi came through here, but I don't know where exactly. The reading isn't precise enough. If we each walk ten feet apart, we'll cover more ground. Look for anything strange."

They spread out, with Kayla and Meera on each end and Henry in the middle. Everyone scanned the ground as they walked.

Violet gasped.

"What is it?" said Benny. "Do you see something?"

Violet bent to grab something. She held it up to show the others. "A plastic water bottle! What's it doing out here?"

Kayla frowned. "You'd think tourists could carry out their garbage."

"I guess we're not the first people to walk this way," Jessie said.

"At least we found it so we can take it back to town." Henry put the bottle in his backpack.

They kept going, and before long, Jessie gave a shout.

"More garbage?" Violet asked.

Jessie crouched in the tall grass. "I don't think so."

The group gathered around, and Jessie handed the thing to Kayla.

"It's the GPS collar!" Kayla examined the thick collar with a small plastic box attached. "This didn't come off by accident. Someone removed it."

"What does it mean?" Benny asked.

Kayla spread her hands. "I'm not sure. Let's get back to the research center. Maybe we can get some more data off the collar."

They hiked back to the truck and loaded up. The drive back was quiet. Everyone was thinking about Tashi. How had her collar come off? If someone removed it, why?

At PAW headquarters, Sonia was working at the computer, but she quickly switched to checking the GPS data. Everyone gathered around the computer as the information loaded.

"Here we go," Sonia said. "Oh, well this is strange. It looks like Tashi was traveling extremely fast right

before her collar turned off."

"Maybe it was chasing something," said Benny.

"Or running away," said Jessie. "Snow leopards are very fast, aren't they?"

"Not this fast," Sonia said. "A snow leopard can sprint at about forty miles per hour. However, that's only for short distances. When they hunt, they sneak up on their prey. They don't need to run far. This data shows the snow leopard picking up speed as it went through the valley. A snow leopard would never run that far at that speed."

"What could it mean?" Jessie wondered.

Benny leaned over the desk. "Maybe we found the world's fastest snow leopard!"

"I wish!" Sonia rubbed a hand over her mouth. "I'm afraid the truth is something worse."

"Maybe the cat was in a vehicle," Henry said. "We were going pretty fast in Meera's truck as we left the valley."

Sonia glanced at him. "That would explain it, and I can't think of anything else that would. The collar traveled at high speed for almost a mile. Then it stood in place for ten minutes before it stopped working altogether."

Henry frowned. "Someone must have caught Tashi. They drove for a little way with the snow leopard in their truck. Then they stopped, took off the collar, and left it behind so they couldn't be tracked."

Kayla put her hands to her cheeks. "This is terrible. I can't believe it happened here under my watch. I shouldn't have gone to Leh."

"It's not your fault," Sonia said. "I was right here in town, and I couldn't stop it. We can't follow the snow leopards around at all times. For one thing, we'd never keep up! For another, we don't want to bother them or change their behavior."

Kayla rubbed her eyes. "I know you're right. I still feel terrible about this." She pulled a chair next to Sonia's, and they talked about what to do next.

Henry waved his siblings to the other side of the room. "We should let them work," he told them.

"Now I feel bad," said Jessie. "Kayla only came to

Leh to pick us up."

"You heard Sonia," Henry replied. "It wouldn't have helped to be here. Anyway, we can't go back and change that. The question is, what can we do now?"

"Do you think that herder man did this?" Benny asked. "Praveer seemed nice, but he didn't like snow leopards. If he thought Tashi killed his animals, he might want to get rid of her."

"He did say he 'was taking care of it,'" said Henry. "I wonder what he meant by that."

Jessie pulled out her notebook and looked at the notes she'd taken. "What about Meera? She said she could make more money by starting a zoo. At first, I thought she was joking, but what if she decided that was a good idea? She might have captured Tashi to show to tourists."

Henry thought about it. "She picked us up in Leh, but that was the day after Tashi's collar stopped working. Meera has the big truck that can drive out in that area, and she has a lot of experience with snow leopards. She'd know how to find one and maybe how to catch it. She would just need a tranquilizer."

"Why wouldn't they take off the collar right away?" Jessie wondered.

"They might have lured Tashi into a cage with meat," Henry said. "The meat would have the tranquilizer in it. Once she was inside, they could drive away, but they couldn't take off the collar until she fell asleep from eating the tranquilizer."

Violet sniffled. "Whatever has happened, I hope Tashi hasn't been hurt."

All the children nodded. "Don't give up hope," Henry said. "Kayla and Sonia are working to figure out what happened. We'll think about it too. We can look around the village and ask questions. If Meera is up to something, maybe someone saw something."

"Let's go," said Benny. "I want to save Tashi."

"Me too," said Violet. "This is bigger than a mystery. It's a mission to save an endangered animal."

CHAPTER 6

Out and About

The children walked through the village toward the lodge. On the way, they caught up with a small cart pulled by a donkey. Henry glanced into the cart as they passed. It held a jumble of scrap metal and tools.

The cart's owner turned as they reached him, and they saw that it was Praveer. They greeted him, and

Violet and Benny went to pet the donkey.

"Children!" He grinned, but his smile faded as he studied the faces of Henry and Jessie. "What is this? You look sad. Are you not enjoying your time in my beautiful homeland?"

"It's not that," Jessie said quickly. "It is beautiful. We got to go up the valley today. We saw the monasteries and blue sheep and even a vulture."

"That is good," Praveer said. "But I can tell something is not right."

"We're okay." Jessie tried to smile. "Just tired. We're not used to the thin air up here."

Praveer nodded. "I have heard this is a problem for foreigners. I do not understand it myself. I have never been farther than Lch. But you Westerners have so much of everything—even air to breathe!"

"We'll feel better after lunch," Henry said.

"Yes!" Benny gave a little bounce. "We'll have a yummy lunch, and then we can work on our mystery."

Praveer looked confused. "What is this mystery?"

"Tashi is missing," Benny said. "She's a snow

leopard. We think someone kidnapped her."

"Kidnapped?" Praveer asked. "I do not know this word."

"We think someone caught her and took her away in a truck," Henry explained.

"Oh my," Praveer said. "That is bad news, but it does happen. Snow leopards are worth a lot of money. Some people still hunt them for their fur."

"Isn't that illegal?" Henry asked.

Praveer bobbed his head. "The law does not stop everyone. Yes, I'm sure that is what happened. Someone must have killed this leopard for its fur. I am sorry it happened, but it is one less problem for me." He gave the children a nod and went on his way.

The children clustered together and watched him walk away. Jessie did not think Praveer sounded very upset about Tashi going missing. And she was surprised at how sure he was that the culprit was after Tashi's fur. Then she noticed something in the back of his cart. "Do you see that?" she whispered. "I think he has an animal trap!"

The trap looked like rusty metal jaws that could snap closed.

Violet gasped. "That would really hurt any animal that got caught in it." She lowered her voice. "Do you think he might have something to do with Tashi going missing?"

Jessie took notes on what had just happened. "His reaction was suspicious," she said. "He doesn't seem to care about snow leopards the way we do."

"I guess as a farmer, he thinks about things differently," Henry said. "Just like Oliver and Meera do."

It was hard to imagine life herding animals in the high mountains. The children had never faced challenges like that. When they had lived in the boxcar, they'd had to find their own food, and Henry had sometimes worried they wouldn't find enough. But they'd never really gone hungry. They had only lived in the woods for a while, in summer. Praveer needed enough food to get his family through long winters in the mountains.

Henry thought about the challenges the herder

faced. "His livestock have a purpose. He uses them for milk and wool and sometimes meat. They're not pets. They are his job, and he has to protect his job."

"That's no excuse for hurting a snow leopard!" Violet cried.

"No," Henry said. "I'm only trying to understand how he might think."

"What should we do?" Jessie asked. "If he did capture Tashi, we may be too late to help her. We might never find out what happened to her."

They all thought for a minute. "Let's find Oliver," Henry said. "He's here to help the snow leopards. Maybe him or his group has some more information about what happened to Tashi."

"He's not staying at our lodge," Jessie said. "How will we find him?"

Henry looked around. "It's a small village. There can't be very many places for people to stay."

The children stopped at some local shops and asked where visitors usually stayed. Not everyone spoke much English. The children wound up pointing and gesturing. It was like a game where they had to act out what they meant and hope people understood.

Finally, after talking to several people, they learned where Oliver might be staying. Besides the lodge, a home at the end of the village rented rooms. The children headed there and found a sign that said Ladakh Mountain Homestay.

"This must be the place." Henry knocked on the door.

No one answered.

"He must be out," Henry said. "I'm surprised no one at all is home."

Benny went to the window and stood on his toes, trying to look in. "It's dark in there."

Jessie joined him. "The curtains are closed, but there's a little gap. I don't see anyone."

"Hey!" The shout came from behind them. They turned to see Oliver hurrying toward them. He stopped and panted for breath. His face was red. He must have been having trouble with the higher altitude too.

"Oh, it's you," Oliver said when he got close. "What are you doing looking in our window?"

Benny grabbed Jessie's hand. Oliver looked upset.

"Looking for you," Henry answered.

Jessie squeezed Benny's hand. "This is like a hotel, right?" she asked. "We thought the front room would be a lobby. We weren't trying to spy on anyone's room."

"Well…okay," Oliver grumbled. "But why did you want to find me?"

"You know Kayla was tracking some of the local snow leopards, right?" Henry asked.

"Of course," Oliver said. "I think it's terrible. No animal should have to wear a GPS collar."

"I'm pretty sure the collars don't hurt the animals," Henry said. "Anyway, a couple of days ago, one of the collars stopped working. We found it yesterday out in the valley. We think someone caught the snow leopard, Tashi, and took her away."

"Oh. Right." Oliver was no longer gasping, but his face was still pink. "Terrible thing—someone catching the snow leopard."

Henry was surprised Oliver didn't seem more upset. "You already heard about it?" he asked.

"I heard about the GPS." Oliver took a deep breath. "I figured it was a poacher. They sell the animals, you know. Snow leopards are worth a lot of money." He paused for another big breath. "I'm sure that's what happened. It's a shame, but we can't do anything about it now."

"There must be something we can do!" Violet didn't want to believe they were too late to help. "Maybe the snow leopard is still somewhere close by."

Oliver shook his head. "That animal is long gone, I'm afraid. It proves people are the cats' biggest problem. That's why my friends and I are here. We've been trying to talk to the local people, but they aren't interested. They don't even try to understand."

"Do you have a translator?" Henry asked. "Some of the locals don't speak much English."

Oliver shrugged and mumbled something. "We're doing important work. We're making a video about the situation. We're going to use it to spread awareness and stop this kind of thing from happening in the future."

"That's great," Jessie said, "but what about now? Tashi might be out there still. She might need our help."

"Sorry, kids." Oliver crossed his arms. "I don't know what else to tell you. Try to convince your friend Kayla to stop doing research on snow leopards. That's probably why this happened, you know?"

Henry scratched his head. "You think poachers got Tashi because PAW is doing research?" he asked. "I don't understand."

"Well, I mean…" Oliver trailed off. He pulled off his mittens and scratched one hand with the other. "People need to stay away from the snow leopards. You don't want them to get used to people. We should leave them entirely alone."

One of Oliver's hands was wrapped in a bulky bandage. It hadn't been that way during the drive to the village. Violet pointed at the hand. "What happened?"

Oliver tucked the injured hand under his other arm.

"Oh, nothing. I slipped and cut it. I was climbing an icy slope, but I'll be fine. Well, I have to get going." He turned and headed back the way he'd come.

The children watched as he hurried away, just like he had the night before.

"He gets hurt a lot," Benny said. "He must be unlucky."

"Or clumsy," Henry said. "He seemed pretty distracted. Maybe he doesn't pay attention to what he's doing."

"He's the opposite of Praveer," Violet said. "Praveer is cheerful and happy to see us, but he doesn't care about snow leopards. Oliver cares about snow leopards, but he's always rushing and is kind of rude."

Jessie was hoping Oliver would help them figure out what was happening. Instead, he only gave them more questions. "Now what?" she asked.

"I wish we knew what happened in that valley," said Violet. "I wish we could go back in time and see it for ourselves."

Henry brightened. "Violet, that's brilliant!"

Benny was confused. "Are you saying we should go back in time?" he asked.

Henry smiled. "In a matter of speaking, yes. I'll explain on the way back to the research center. I think I know how we can find out what happened to Tashi."

CHAPTER 7

A Call for Help

Back at the research center, Kayla and Sonia were leaning back in their chairs.

"I just don't know—" Sonia broke off in the middle of her sentence as the children came in.

Kayla managed to smile, though she still didn't look happy. "Back so soon? Did you get lunch?"

Benny stepped forward and spoke firmly. "This is

even more important than lunch!"

Kayla's eyebrows went up. "Then it must be pretty important."

"We were thinking about the trail cam footage," Henry said. "Have you reviewed it yet?"

"Oh, that's right." Kayla grabbed her backpack from the floor. "I almost forgot that I collected the memory cards." She pulled them out of the pack. "Why?"

"It can bring us back in time!" said Benny.

Kayla looked puzzled, so Henry explained. "We wanted to see the footage from the day Tashi's collar stopped working. Maybe the trail camera will show who was there that day."

"Of course! They might not show the exact place where Tashi went missing, but there might be a clue." Kayla slid the memory card into the reader. "I was so focused on the GPS data that I didn't even think about the cameras."

Jessie sat down at the desk. She was the best with computers, and she knew just what they were looking for. "Let's see. Tashi disappeared two days ago.

There are a number of videos from that day."

She started working her way through the videos. One showed a fox. Another showed something at the very edge of the screen. They played the video at slow speed but still couldn't figure out what the thing was.

When the next video played, everyone gasped as a snow leopard came down the crevice. "That's Tashi," Sonia said. "She's still wearing her collar."

The snow leopard passed out of the camera's range. They didn't see any people.

"We know she was okay that morning," said Kayla.

Jessie played the rest of the videos from the memory card. They didn't show anything interesting.

"I guess that's no help," Henry said.

"Not necessarily," said Kayla. "That camera looks toward the crevice. It only shows who goes up and down there." Kayla ejected the memory card and put in another. "This is from a camera that looks into the valley. The one facing up gives us the best close-ups of animals traveling through the crevice. This has a wider view."

Jessie started playing videos. They saw the fox heading downhill, with a herd of sheep in the valley below.

Sonia leaned closer to the computer and squinted. "I think those are wild sheep. The herders aren't supposed to let their animals graze in that area. Some of the nomads don't know that though."

"No-mads?" Benny asked. "Are those people who never get mad?"

Sonia laughed. "I wish we had more people who never got mad, Benny. But these are *nomads*—one word. It means people who don't live in a single place. They travel from place to place, like herders who move around to find fresh food for their livestock. Around here, they live in big tents, which they roll up, put on their yaks, and bring to wherever the grass is fresh."

"Oh. That sounds nice." Benny thought for a minute. "Maybe only in summer though. Unless they can go to the beach in winter."

"We're pretty far from any beaches," Henry said, mussing his brother's hair.

"Are there any more videos from the second camera?" Violet asked.

"Yes, we still have a couple of hours before the collar stopped working," Kayla said. "This next video is getting closer, Jessie."

Jessie hit play.

"What's that?" Henry leaned over Jessie's shoulder. He could see something moving through the trees. It was bigger than an animal and much faster.

"A truck!" said Benny.

Jessie paused the video. "I don't recognize it."

"I don't either," Sonia said.

The large truck was green with a patch of white on the side. It was large with oversize wheels. "It's like the one Meera drives," Violet said. "Only hers was white with the leopard painted in black. Maybe the white on this one is something like that, a logo."

Jessie started the video again. The truck moved out of the camera's view. They didn't see Tashi, or any snow leopard, before the video ended.

"It shows us that someone was in the area," Kayla

said. "It doesn't prove they captured Tashi. Let's keep going. The first camera showed Tashi going down the ravine an hour before dusk. This camera should catch her as well."

They found a video showing Tashi. She passed in front of the camera and turned downhill. Then her thick, fluffy tail waved as she bounded out of sight.

Two videos later they saw the truck again. It was heading back toward the village.

Kayla watched that video once more. "The truck is suspicious. They were in the valley when Tashi came down. It still wouldn't be easy to catch her. It wouldn't even be easy to see her."

"Some of the locals are good at spotting snow leopards," Sonia said. "It's amazing. They'll point to a jumble of rocks, and even with binoculars it takes me a couple minutes to see the cat."

"Does that mean it was someone from the village?" Violet asked. She didn't want it to be Praveer.

"I don't know," Sonia said.

"We haven't seen many vehicles in the village,"

Henry said. "In fact, I only remember seeing Meera's truck, the van parked by the lodge, and Praveer's cart. We haven't seen anything that looks like that truck."

"Didn't Meera say she has two trucks?" said Benny. "Maybe the other one is green with a white leopard."

Kayla and Sonia looked at each other.

"I've only seen her white truck," Kayla said. "Why would she trap Tashi? Snow leopard tours are big business for her."

"Meera joked about opening a zoo," Henry said. "Maybe she decided that would be easier to keep a leopard than to find them on her tours. She could charge extra to see one."

Kayla looked unsure. "Do you think Meera would do that, Sonia?"

Sonia shook her head. "I don't," she said. "But time might be running out. We should at least check it out. She parks her vehicles in a big shed here in the village."

Benny bounced up and down. "Let's go see if the green truck is there!"

Kayla and Sonia grabbed their coats, and the group headed back outside. Sonia moved quickly until she realized the children couldn't keep up. They still weren't used to the thin air. She stopped and waited for them.

Jessie laughed. "I want to run, but I can't. My mind is in a hurry, but my body wants to go slow."

Kayla patted her shoulder. "We'll get there. It's not far now. See the tan building with the metal roof?"

"If Meera has Tashi, she won't hurt the snow leopard," Henry said. "We have time."

Violet led the way forward. "I still want to hurry."

A faint shriek cut through the air. Kayla jerked to a stop. "Shh. Listen!"

Everyone froze and listened as the sound came again. "Yee-ow! Yee-ow!"

They listened for a couple more seconds without hearing anything else.

"That sounded like the scream we heard last night," Jessie said.

"Maybe Oliver hurt himself again." Violet giggled. "I feel bad, but he's really clumsy."

Kayla looked between the children. "What are you talking about?"

"Oliver," said Jessie. "The man we rode here with. We heard that noise last night when he was in the street. He'd stubbed his toe."

Kayla shook her head. "I don't know what you heard last night, but the sound we just heard was not Oliver. That was a snow leopard."

The children stared at her. "Snow leopards make that sound?" Violet asked.

Kayla nodded. "That was definitely a snow leopard. They can't roar like other big cats. Their call is more of a high-pitched scream or yowl."

Jessie frowned. "It sounded a lot like the sound we heard Oliver make last night. Am I remembering wrong?"

"It only happened once last night," Henry said. "But I think so. Kayla, didn't you hear it?"

"I fell asleep pretty early," said Kayla. "I don't know what you heard, but I'm sure that was a snow leopard just now."

Sonia nodded her agreement. "Their calls can be heard for quite a distance, but that was especially loud. It sounded like it was near the village."

"Meera's garage?" Violet pointed ahead to their destination. "Let's go see!"

The excitement gave the children extra energy. Even with the thin air, they hurried to see if they had found their missing snow leopard.

CHAPTER 8

Out in the Open

Meera's main building had three garage doors, each big enough for a large truck to go through. A smaller building the size of a shed sat to one side. Meera stood in the open doorway of that building, looking around.

The Aldens huffed for air as they approached her. Before they could catch their breaths and start to question her, Meera said, "Did you hear that noise? It sounded like a snow leopard."

The children looked at one another. Did this mean Meera didn't have Tashi? Or was it a trick to make them *think* she didn't have the big cat?

"It was a snow leopard." Kayla put her hands on her hips. "We believe someone captured Tashi using a truck. Meera, was it you?"

Meera laughed. "Me? Why would I want to catch a snow leopard?"

Kayla bit her lip, looking uncertain.

"You said you could make more money opening a zoo," Benny said. "Maybe you wanted Tashi so you could show her to people."

Meera laughed again. "That was a joke!" She dabbed at her eyes. "If I tried to open a zoo with a snow leopard, I would go to jail."

"Not if you kept it a secret," said Violet.

Meera shook her head. "I like giving tours, and my tours do well enough. I don't need to risk breaking the law."

"That makes sense." Sonia smiled. "But, Meera, would you mind if we take a look in your garage?"

Meera crossed her arms. "Huh. You still think I might steal a leopard." She shook her head. "Put Tashi in a cage? No way! But you can search. Go ahead."

"You're sure?" Sonia asked.

Meera went to the garage and hauled open one of the doors. "I insist! You have to see that I'm telling the truth. No one will call *me* a poacher."

Sonia stayed to talk to Meera. She waved Kayla and the children into the garage.

They paused just inside the large space. Light poured in from the open door behind them, leaving the far corners dark. Kayla glanced back and spoke quietly. "We want to stay friendly with Meera. We need her as a guide. Sonia will smooth things over while we look around."

"There are the two white trucks," Henry said. "I don't see a green truck like the one in the video."

"We should still look around," said Jessie.

The children walked carefully through the garage, pausing to admire a line of snowmobiles. Beside one, in the back corner of the garage, a sheet was draped over something large.

Henry carefully approached the dark corner of the garage. Underneath the sheet, he thought he saw something move. Could there be a cage underneath?

"Do you see something, Henry?" Kayla called.

"I don't know," Henry said. Then in one motion, he yanked the sheet up. A cloud of dust flew in the air, blocking his view.

When the dust cleared, he saw that it was not a cage after all. Instead, a large stack of boxes sat in front of him. On top, a mouse was frozen in fear.

The children breathed a sigh of relief as they headed outside. Wherever Tashi was, she wasn't in Meera's garage.

Meera crossed her arms. "See? I didn't do anything illegal."

"We know that now," Kayla said. "I'm sorry we questioned you, but I'm glad to prove you right."

They said goodbye and headed back into the village.

"Now what?" Jessie asked. "I'm happy it wasn't Meera who took Tashi, but if not her, who could it be?"

A woman passed by on the street with several large animals. They looked like heavy cows with shaggy fur and curved horns that ended in sharp points. Kayla pulled the children to the side so the woman could pass.

Violet watched the animals with wide eyes. "What are those?"

"Those are yaks," Sonia said. "They're a kind of cattle, but they do better than cows in this environment. Yaks can handle the cold and high altitude."

"Like Tashi," Violet said. For a moment, everyone was silent as the woman with the yaks passed.

"Meera could still have Tashi somewhere else," Kayla said at last, "but it doesn't seem likely. She's right; she'd risk too much trouble if she tried to keep a leopard hidden. For Meera, the best place for a snow leopard is in the wild."

"Could we have heard some other snow leopard?" Henry asked. "Maybe one of them came close to town to hunt."

"I doubt it," Sonia said. "I've never heard a call that loud when I was in the village. Besides, snow leopards are most active at dawn and dusk, not midday."

Kayla sighed. "I feel like we're so close," she said, "but short of knocking on people's doors, I don't know what to do." Then she managed to smile. "You kids still haven't had lunch. Why don't you go back to the lodge? Norboo will feed you."

Benny hated to see anyone go hungry. "What about you?"

"We have some snacks at the research center," Kayla said. "We'll let you know if we can come up with anything more about Tashi." She and Sonia waved and headed off to the PAW building.

The children started back toward the lodge, following the woman with the yaks. The big animals moved slowly, which was fine for the Aldens. They had a lot to think about.

"Kayla seemed to think it could be anyone," said Jessie. "But I don't think most villagers know or care too much about the snow leopards. To them, they are probably just part of daily life."

Henry nodded. "But not to everyone," he said. "Some people, like those who raise animals, probably think about them a lot."

"Like Praveer," said Jessie. She thought back to the conversation they'd had with the herder. He was nice, but he definitely did not like snow leopards.

"Didn't Praveer say he lived just up the road?" asked Benny.

Henry nodded. "The sound of that yowl might have carried that far," he said. "Not to mention Praveer had an animal trap in the back of his cart."

Violet cringed at the thought. "If he did capture Tashi in that horrible trap, she's probably hurt."

Jessie put her arm around her sister. "At least we heard a snow leopard today. Sonia said that it was probably Tashi that we heard. That means she's alive and hasn't been taken away."

"Okay." Violet felt a little better. "Can we try to find Praveer though?"

"That's a good idea." Henry pointed toward a mountain peak. "When he said he lived five minutes outside the village, he pointed that way. Let's get some lunch and then see if we can find his farm. I think Praveer is our next suspect."

❖

After lunch, the children walked out of the village. It wasn't hard to spot Praveer's home. They walked through tall yellow grass toward a white building with a thatched roof. Praveer stood outside next to a wall of large stones that formed a corral. The children waved and called out as they approached.

Praveer turned and waved back. "Hello, children! You're coming to visit me? How nice."

The stone wall was only about two and a half feet

high. Violet looked over it. She didn't see any animals in the corral.

"Where is your herd?" she asked.

Praveer looked out over the empty corral. "My sons have the animals out grazing." He picked up a metal bar about five feet long and pounded one end into the ground outside the stone wall. "It is a good thing. The past few days have been very busy."

Henry looked around the corral. It certainly didn't look like much was going on at the farm. "Is that a fence you're building?" Henry asked.

Praveer nodded. "I've decided to upgrade. I need to make sure my fence is tall enough. Especially now..." Praveer looked nervously back toward his house.

Jessie followed his eyes toward the building with the thatched roof. "Why do you say that?" she asked. Something about the empty corral and tall fence made her nervous. Could Praveer be planning to keep a snow leopard in the corral?

Before Praveer could answer Jessie's question, a cry

rang out from the house. The first noise sounded like it came from a human. The second sound definitely came from an animal.

Without saying another word, Praveer took off running toward the house.

The Aldens followed quickly but carefully. "Didn't Praveer say that his sons had taken all of the animals out grazing?" asked Jessie. "If so, where was that noise coming from?"

Henry shook his head. "I don't know. Let's check it out."

As they approached the house, the children heard stomping and banging coming from inside. It sounded like something was on the loose—something big.

"Grab its legs!" said Praveer. "Do not let her get out the door!"

There was a scramble within. Suddenly the door flung open, and an animal burst out. It was shaggy with a large head and two small horns.

"A baby yak!" said Henry.

"Don't let her get away!" said Praveer.

Henry bent down and corralled the yak. Even though it looked very young, it still almost knocked him over. Praveer helped Henry steer the young animal toward the empty corral.

"She's so cute," said Violet. "Why was she being kept in your house?"

Praveer closed the gate on the corral. "This is what I was trying to tell you. It has been very busy here the last few days. Our young yak has been sick. My wife and I have been doing all we can to nurse it to health." He looked fondly at the little animal. "It's only now that it has gotten healthy enough to get up and run on its own."

Still Jessie had more questions. "Why are you building a fence now?" she asked.

"The larger fence is to keep out wild animals like leopards," he said. "With a newborn it's even more important that I do this."

Henry remembered what Praveer had said about taking care of his leopard problem. His solution was a taller fence! "We thought you might have something to do with the disappearance of the snow leopard," Henry said.

Praveer gave a friendly laugh. "I have come to accept the snow leopards. But that doesn't mean I can't try and protect my herd from them. Would you like to come inside, and we can talk more?"

Benny and Violet looked at Henry. They wouldn't normally go into a stranger's house. But how often did they have a chance to see the inside of a home in the Himalayas?

"I think it's okay this time," Henry told them quietly. "I told Norboo who we were visiting. He said Praveer is well respected in the village."

They went inside and met Praveer's wife. She wore a loose black dress tied with a blue cloth belt. She had black hair streaked with gray, pulled into a ponytail. She was still tidying up from the baby yak getting loose.

They sat on low cushions. Colorful carpets covered the floor. Wooden beams supported the ceiling and narrow windows gave a view outside. Praveer's wife made hot butter tea. It was thick and creamy. The children were still not used to the taste, but they were grateful for a warm drink on a chilly day.

Jessie no longer believed Praveer was a suspect. Still, she had some questions for him. "Do you own a truck?" she asked.

"No. I do not drive." Praveer laughed. "Where would I go? I only go into the village or into the fields with the herd. One or two times a year I get a ride to Leh for supplies."

Henry thought back to when they had seen Praveer in town. "We saw an animal trap in your cart," he said. "We were afraid you might use it to catch a snow leopard."

"I would not do that," Praveer said. "That old trap is one my father left behind. My father and grandfather used to trap the cats to keep them away. They did not know better. Today we do. The snow leopards are part of what makes my home beautiful. We do not want to lose them. And I hope that you can find the one that is missing."

After the children were done with their tea, they thanked Praveer and his wife and headed back to the village.

"I'm glad Praveer wasn't the culprit," said Violet. "Still, we aren't any closer to finding Tashi. I'm worried that we're running out of time."

"Are we sure that sound we heard was a snow leopard?" Benny asked. "Maybe it really was Oliver again. Maybe he sounds like a snow leopard when he hurts himself. Yee-ow!"

Violet and Jessie laughed at Benny's imitation.

Henry turned serious. "Maybe we're looking at it backward," he said. "If what we heard today was a snow leopard, maybe what we heard last night wasn't Oliver after all. Maybe that was a snow leopard too."

"So the snow leopard yelled at the same time Oliver stubbed his toe?" said Benny.

Jessie gasped. "Or Oliver lied about stubbing his toe."

"It does seem suspicious now," Henry said. "And yesterday, he got mad when he saw us at the place he's staying. Then he didn't even go inside. He turned around and went back the way he came."

"He seems to care about the animals," said Violet. "But he doesn't listen to anyone else. Do you think he would go so far as to capture one to try and protect it?"

"I don't know," said Henry. "But I think we have one more suspect to investigate."

CHAPTER 9

Adding It Up

The children headed to the guesthouse at the edge of town. This time, they did not need to search for Oliver. The young activist was hurrying outside, carrying his luggage.

A thin young woman followed him.

"We're not leaving for hours," she said. "What's your hurry?"

Oliver shrugged. "Just anxious to get on the road."

"More like anxious to get away from things." The woman went back into the building.

The children walked toward Oliver. "Are you leaving?" Henry asked.

"Oh, hello." Oliver pushed his luggage against the wall. "We're leaving tonight."

"Do you think you did some good here?" Jessie asked.

"We sure did something! Your friend Kayla wouldn't listen to me, but—" Oliver broke off.

"But what?" Henry asked.

Oliver shrugged. "Well, we do what we have to do. Not everyone will listen."

"Okay." Henry wasn't sure what that meant. Did Oliver decide he'd never convince PAW to stop their research? Maybe he'd thought he'd accomplish more somewhere else. "Is Meera giving you a ride back to Leh?" Henry asked.

"No, we're going to another village." Oliver checked the time. "A friend is coming in his truck.

We want to be ready so we can load up and go when he gets here."

Benny looked like he was about to say something. Jessie put a hand on his shoulder and squeezed. "What does the truck look like?" she asked. "We can watch for it. There aren't many trucks in the village."

"It's dark green," Oliver said.

Jessie tried to hide her excitement. "All green? Does it have any other colors?"

"It has a white symbol on the door," Oliver said. "The back is covered."

Jessie and Henry exchanged looks. That sounded like the truck from the trail cam. What was Oliver's friend doing in the valley the day Tashi disappeared?

Benny's eyes were big. Jessie had warned him to be quiet, so he pressed his lips together. He wanted to get away so they could talk.

"Well, bye." Oliver opened the door to the guesthouse.

"Are you feeling any better since your fall?" Violet asked.

Oliver paused and looked back. "What?"

"The fall where you cut your hand." Violet pointed at the bandage on Oliver's hand.

"Oh, right." He turned and looked at them all. "Yes, much better. It was just a scratch—I mean a cut. Thanks. Well, see you kids around."

"Did you hurt yourself again today?" Jessie asked before he could go inside. "We heard a scream a little while ago."

"A scream?" Oliver looked confused. "I didn't hear anyone screaming."

"It was like this," Benny said. "Yee-ow, yee-ow!"

"Oh, right." Oliver scratched his bandaged hand. "Yeah. That's exactly what happened. I stubbed my toe."

"Again?" Henry and Jessie said together.

"Again?" Oliver frowned. "What do you mean?"

Jessie put her hands on her hips. "You said you stubbed your toe last night. So you stubbed your toe twice and hurt your hand falling on ice? All in two days?"

Oliver glanced into the building. "Um, I'm pretty clumsy." He gave a weak laugh.

The children stepped toward Oliver. "No one is that clumsy," Violet said.

"You didn't make that sound," Henry said. "That yell was from a snow leopard. Sonia and Meera both said so. They would know."

Oliver's mouth opened and closed.

"Why would you say you made those sounds?" Jessie asked. "Is it because you didn't want us to know it was an upset snow leopard? Maybe your hand wasn't hurt from falling on ice either. Maybe it was from catching a wild animal who scratched you."

Oliver pulled the door closed, cutting off the sounds from inside. He sank to the ground and put his hands over his face.

Jessie crouched in front of him. "Did you capture Tashi and remove her collar?"

Oliver nodded without looking up. "My group wanted to get the radio collar off," he said quietly. "We don't think wild animals should have collars or tags."

Henry leaned over him. "I thought you wanted people to leave wild animals alone."

"I do!" Oliver looked up at all of them. "I got here after they captured the cat. They told me to keep it sedated, or asleep, while they tried to find more snow leopards. They wanted to take all the cats we found to a more remote area where they wouldn't be bothered."

"But snow leopards have territory," Violet said. "This is Tashi's home!"

"Yeah." Oliver sighed deeply. "I joined this group because they wanted to help animals. But I think they went too far."

"They sure did!" Jessie snapped. "You thought people were bothering Tashi, so you captured her? You're going to move her to a strange new place away from her home? You're the ones bothering her."

"I know." Oliver stood up. "We didn't follow our own beliefs. I think everyone got carried away. I know I did."

"You're very lucky," Violet said. "Handling wild

animals is dangerous. It doesn't sound like anyone in your group is an expert. You could've gotten hurt a lot worse."

"You're right." Oliver trembled. "That cat is not happy about being in a cage. I felt terrible keeping her sedated, so I skipped the dose. She woke up enough to scratch me. I should never have gotten involved with this plan."

Oliver lowered his voice. "Now I don't know what to do. Everyone will get mad at me if I tell them we made a mistake. I don't think they'll listen."

The children looked at one another. They knew where Tashi was and why she'd been captured. Now they had to make sure she got released safely.

"We'll tell Kayla what happened," Henry said. "Will you stay here and keep quiet? I'm sure we can get you help, but we need some time."

Oliver gave a deep sigh of relief. "Thank you. Yes, I'll make sure they don't leave with the cat before you get back. I'll turn in the rest of the group. And myself." He took another deep breath and let it out.

"I'm scared. I don't want to be arrested! Especially in a place far from home. But even that is better than taking that poor snow leopard away from her home."

"You're doing the right thing now," Violet said. Oliver had made a big mistake, but at least he was willing to fix things.

The children hurried back to PAW headquarters. They explained everything to Kayla and Sonia.

Sonia got on the satellite radio and called the wildlife police. "They're sending a team," she said.

"Will they arrive in time?" Violet asked.

"The local police are on the way too," said Sonia. "They'll make sure the thieves don't leave town. Then the wildlife police will take over."

"How long do you think it will take?" Benny asked. "Tashi needs to get back out to the mountains. And I don't want to miss dinner!"

Kayla laughed. "You kids should go back to the lodge. It will take some time to sort everything out. I'll let you know as soon as it's over."

The children grumbled a little at missing out.

On the other hand, it had been a long day in the thin air. They were tired.

On the way back to the lodge, the Aldens saw that the police were already on the scene. Oliver was being led away, and the others from his group were detained nearby.

The children kept their distance, even though they wanted to know what was going to happen to the spotted leopard.

"I won't be able to relax until we know Tashi is safe," said Violet.

"I won't either," said Henry. "Still, there's not much we can do. We have to leave everything to the experts."

"You know what will make us feel better?" Benny skipped ahead. "A nice big dinner."

At the hotel, the children tried to relax. Jessie caught up on her notes. Violet sketched. Henry and Benny helped Norboo prepare dinner. They started with steamed dumplings stuffed with vegetables and cheese. Then they made warm vegetable soup and bread. Benny was right: a good

meal did make them feel better.

They were eating dessert when Kayla arrived. She sank onto one of the low, cushioned seats. "Thank goodness that's over. Tashi looks fine, just annoyed. She will get a complete checkup before we let her go tomorrow."

"And food too, right?" Benny asked. "Maybe she won't be so annoyed once she has dinner."

Kayla grinned. "Yes, Sonia is getting Tashi food now. She won't go hungry."

"She'll be so glad to be back home," Violet said. "It's hard to believe she's been in the village this whole time. We still haven't even seen a snow leopard!"

Kayla smiled. "I can't let you leave without that happening," she said. "Get some sleep tonight. Tomorrow we are going to see Tashi where she belongs—in the wild."

CHAPTER 10

Returning Home

The next morning, Kayla and the children met Meera and Sonia outside the lodge. Meera waved them over to her truck. "Hurry! They are ready to go."

"Where is Tashi?" Violet asked.

"She's in the other truck," Kayla said. "The wildlife department is in charge now."

They followed the first truck down a winding road

into the valley. Kayla used a radio to let the wildlife warden know when they were in Tashi's territory, and both trucks parked near the crevice Tashi liked to use.

The children piled out of the truck, and the people from the other vehicle opened the back end. They lifted down a large cage. Inside, a spotted cat hunched down, looking around suspiciously. Her body was more than four feet long, and her thick tail added another three feet.

Violet clapped her hands together. "Oh, she is beautiful."

"She has a new radio collar," Henry noted.

"Yes," Kayla said. "We will be able to continue our research. The veterinarian did a full exam. Tashi was a little low in calcium, so they gave her a supplement. Now, she'll be healthier than ever."

A man in the other group called out something.

"Stand back now," Sonia said. "They're going to release her."

The wildlife experts had attached a rope to the cage door. The rope allowed them to stand away from the cage as they opened it. Tashi crept out and crouched on the grass. She spent a minute looking around then loped forward.

Kayla and the Aldens gathered around the cage to get a closer look as the leopard moved away.

Tashi paused at the steep slope at the base of the mountain and gave one glance back. The she darted uphill in powerful, quick bounds before disappearing into the crevice.

Violet let out the breath she'd been holding. "That was amazing."

"This whole visit has been amazing," Henry said. "I'm sorry we're leaving so soon."

Jessie nodded. "I finally feel like I can catch my breath at this altitude."

Benny wrinkled his nose. "If we stay another week, I might get used to that funny yak butter tea."

The others laughed.

"Things are definitely different here," Kayla said.

"I'm going to miss it." Jessie took a deep breath of the cool mountain air. "The scenery is wonderful.

The mountains are so high and rugged. We got to see blue sheep that aren't blue, vultures, and even a snow leopard. But I think my favorite part was meeting the people. Can we say goodbye to Praveer before we go?"

"I know his farm," Meera said. "We will stop on the way back."

They said goodbye to the wildlife authorities and piled into the truck with Meera, Kayla, and Sonia. On the way to the village, Meera stopped by Praveer's farm. Praveer came out to greet them.

"You finished the new corral," Henry said. He watched as the baby yak trotted around the edge of the corral.

"Yes," said Praveer. "Now my animals will be safe."

Kayla studied the new fence. "You can get lights for the top that will turn on if an animal comes close. That will also help scare away predators."

Violet frowned. "I know it's important to keep predators away from farm animals. But you said the snow leopards eat farm animals when they can't find their usual food. If they can't get to the livestock, will they go hungry?"

"They would normally eat ibex and wild sheep," Kayla said. "We have to make sure they have enough of that wild game. Some land has been set aside for those animals instead of livestock."

"So if they have enough wild prey, they won't eat livestock?" Violet asked.

"Well, most of us would rather have an easy meal than a hard one," Kayla said. "We make sure the snow leopards have enough wild game." She pointed at the high fence. "Then we don't make it too easy for them to get to the livestock. It's better for everyone if they hunt wild prey."

"That makes sense." Jessie had her pencil ready to take more notes. "What else can people do?"

"In some places, there are programs to pay farmers who lose animals to snow leopards," Kayla said. "Then farmers are less likely to kill the leopards. They know they won't lose money if a leopard kills one of their animals."

"There are also groups that help people find different ways to make money," Sonia said. "They train people for new jobs. Like tourism. Right, Meera?"

Meera nodded. "Tourists pay a lot of money to visit. Sometimes the money all goes to outside companies, but it should stay here. Tour companies should use local guides."

"Many villages have converted homes into lodges where travelers can stay," Sonia added, "which also creates jobs."

"It also means visitors get to know local people," Henry said. "I'm glad we did. We'd better head back and pack up though. Meera, you are driving us back to Leh, right?"

"Yes. And I will pick up another group there too. I'll tell them my friends saw a snow leopard this morning." She grinned. "This is a great business."

They said goodbye to Praveer and returned to the village. They dropped Sonia at the research center. She wanted to make sure Tashi's radio collar was transmitting its signal. Then they went to the lodge.

Jessie finished first and looked out the window. "This is a beautiful view. I really will miss it."

Violet took a picture of her sister at the window. "This will help us remember. I loved seeing Tashi and the other animals, but I think I'm ready to go home now. I want to see Grandfather and Watch."

Jessie turned from the window. "Watch has probably been looking everywhere for us. I can't wait to see him again."

Benny nodded. "The best adventures are the ones where you go home after."

Kayla helped the children with their bags and led the way to the truck. As Meera stowed the luggage in the back, Kayla said, "I'm going to miss you kids, but I'm glad you came. I thought I would teach you about Ladakh and snow leopards, but you did more than just learn. You helped make sure Tashi stays wild."

Violet hugged her. "We'll miss you too. I want to go home, but I don't want the adventure to be over."

"Oh, don't worry about that. I think we can all

use a rest after this week. But your grandfather and I have been talking." Kayla winked. "We have a lot of summer left. Plenty of time for more adventures."

Benny bounced up and down. "Like what? Is it a surprise?"

"Will we get to help more animals?" Violet asked.

"Will we learn about new places and people?" Jessie wondered.

"Whatever it is, I know it will be fun," Henry said.

Kayla just grinned. "Come on. Load up."

They piled into the truck, chatting happily. Their time in India might be ending, but their adventures were far from over.

Turn the page for a sneak preview of

Mystery of the Vanishing Forest

the next book in the
Endangered Animals series.

After a long drive into the rain forest, Kayla stopped the car and parked next to a stake by the road. "See the marker?" she said. "The area behind us has been surveyed, but not the area in front of us. So we'll start here."

"What will happen if we find orangutan nests in this area?" Violet asked.

"If we can show that orangutans live in this area," said Kayla, "we might be able to get more of the rain forest protected. We'll move together in a line. If you see a nest, call out and stop, and I'll come over and record the location before we move on."

She handed out binoculars, and the group started their survey. It didn't take long before Jessie spotted the first nest, and soon after, Benny saw one too.

Violet, who was on one end of the line, really

wanted to find a nest. She knew that protecting more of the rain forest meant protecting all of the endangered animals that lived there. She looked carefully up to her right, where no one else was walking. Something seemed strange. The forest growth didn't look as thick in that direction. She could see the sunlight coming down through the trees.

"It looks like there aren't as many plants over there," Violet said. "Does that mean there's a road or a trail?"

"There isn't supposed to be anything that way except more forest," Kayla said. "That's odd."

"We should go look," Henry said.

Kayla agreed. She marked where they left off with a branch, and they walked toward the place Violet had noticed. As they got closer, they could see the area had fewer plants. The larger ones had been crushed down.

"This is too big to be an animal trail," Jessie said.

Henry pointed down to the ground. "And there

are tire tracks. That's why these plants are crushed. Something drove over them."

"Should we investigate?" Jessie asked.

"Yes," said Kayla. "I don't like this. No one should be driving off the road."

The air was heavy and hot as they followed the tire marks. It was also very quiet.

"Why aren't we hearing any birds?" Violet asked.

"Maybe we scared them off," Henry said. "Though we didn't seem to scare them earlier."

Kayla, who was leading the way, stopped suddenly. "Oh no!" she said.

As the Aldens caught up with her, they saw what had upset her.

There was no more forest. All the trees and other plants had been cut down. The remains of an orangutan nest spilled out from the branches of a downed tree. The far side of the clearing ran right up to the fence of the farm they had visited earlier.

"Why would someone do this?" Violet asked.

Kayla wiped her forehead as she looked around

in dismay. "I don't know," she said. "It may be illegal loggers."

"Or the farm is expanding," Jessie said.

Kayla crossed her arms. "They can't do that. They know the boundary to their property and that any forest on this side doesn't belong to them."

Suddenly, Benny grabbed hold of Jessie's arm. In a loud whisper, he said, "There's a man over there!"

Across the clearing, they could see someone standing with his back to them, looking up into a tree. Did the person have something to do with the clear-cut forest?

"We'd better go back to the car. We need to report this right away," Kayla said. She looked back at the figure in the forest. "Let's be quiet when we leave."

THE BOXCAR CHILDREN® MYSTERIES

THE BOXCAR CHILDREN
SURPRISE ISLAND
THE YELLOW HOUSE MYSTERY
MYSTERY RANCH
MIKE'S MYSTERY
BLUE BAY MYSTERY
THE WOODSHED MYSTERY
THE LIGHTHOUSE MYSTERY
MOUNTAIN TOP MYSTERY
SCHOOLHOUSE MYSTERY
CABOOSE MYSTERY
HOUSEBOAT MYSTERY
SNOWBOUND MYSTERY
TREE HOUSE MYSTERY
BICYCLE MYSTERY
MYSTERY IN THE SAND
MYSTERY BEHIND THE WALL
BUS STATION MYSTERY
BENNY UNCOVERS A MYSTERY
THE HAUNTED CABIN MYSTERY
THE DESERTED LIBRARY MYSTERY
THE ANIMAL SHELTER MYSTERY
THE OLD MOTEL MYSTERY
THE MYSTERY OF THE HIDDEN PAINTING
THE AMUSEMENT PARK MYSTERY
THE MYSTERY OF THE MIXED-UP ZOO
THE CAMP-OUT MYSTERY
THE MYSTERY GIRL
THE MYSTERY CRUISE
THE DISAPPEARING FRIEND MYSTERY
THE MYSTERY OF THE SINGING GHOST
THE MYSTERY IN THE SNOW
THE PIZZA MYSTERY
THE MYSTERY HORSE
THE MYSTERY AT THE DOG SHOW
THE CASTLE MYSTERY
THE MYSTERY OF THE LOST VILLAGE
THE MYSTERY ON THE ICE
THE MYSTERY OF THE PURPLE POOL
THE GHOST SHIP MYSTERY
THE MYSTERY IN WASHINGTON, DC
THE CANOE TRIP MYSTERY
THE MYSTERY OF THE HIDDEN BEACH
THE MYSTERY OF THE MISSING CAT
THE MYSTERY AT SNOWFLAKE INN
THE MYSTERY ON STAGE

THE DINOSAUR MYSTERY
THE MYSTERY OF THE STOLEN MUSIC
THE MYSTERY AT THE BALL PARK
THE CHOCOLATE SUNDAE MYSTERY
THE MYSTERY OF THE HOT AIR BALLOON
THE MYSTERY BOOKSTORE
THE PILGRIM VILLAGE MYSTERY
THE MYSTERY OF THE STOLEN BOXCAR
THE MYSTERY IN THE CAVE
THE MYSTERY ON THE TRAIN
THE MYSTERY AT THE FAIR
THE MYSTERY OF THE LOST MINE
THE GUIDE DOG MYSTERY
THE HURRICANE MYSTERY
THE PET SHOP MYSTERY
THE MYSTERY OF THE SECRET MESSAGE
THE FIREHOUSE MYSTERY
THE MYSTERY IN SAN FRANCISCO
THE NIAGARA FALLS MYSTERY
THE MYSTERY AT THE ALAMO
THE OUTER SPACE MYSTERY
THE SOCCER MYSTERY
THE MYSTERY IN THE OLD ATTIC
THE GROWLING BEAR MYSTERY
THE MYSTERY OF THE LAKE MONSTER
THE MYSTERY AT PEACOCK HALL
THE WINDY CITY MYSTERY
THE BLACK PEARL MYSTERY
THE CEREAL BOX MYSTERY
THE PANTHER MYSTERY
THE MYSTERY OF THE QUEEN'S JEWELS
THE STOLEN SWORD MYSTERY
THE BASKETBALL MYSTERY
THE MOVIE STAR MYSTERY
THE MYSTERY OF THE PIRATE'S MAP
THE GHOST TOWN MYSTERY
THE MYSTERY OF THE BLACK RAVEN
THE MYSTERY IN THE MALL
THE MYSTERY IN NEW YORK
THE GYMNASTICS MYSTERY
THE POISON FROG MYSTERY
THE MYSTERY OF THE EMPTY SAFE
THE HOME RUN MYSTERY
THE GREAT BICYCLE RACE MYSTERY
THE MYSTERY OF THE WILD PONIES
THE MYSTERY IN THE COMPUTER GAME

THE HONEYBEE MYSTERY
THE MYSTERY AT THE CROOKED HOUSE
THE HOCKEY MYSTERY
THE MYSTERY OF THE MIDNIGHT DOG
THE MYSTERY OF THE SCREECH OWL
THE SUMMER CAMP MYSTERY
THE COPYCAT MYSTERY
THE HAUNTED CLOCK TOWER MYSTERY
THE MYSTERY OF THE TIGER'S EYE
THE DISAPPEARING STAIRCASE MYSTERY
THE MYSTERY ON BLIZZARD MOUNTAIN
THE MYSTERY OF THE SPIDER'S CLUE
THE CANDY FACTORY MYSTERY
THE MYSTERY OF THE MUMMY'S CURSE
THE MYSTERY OF THE STAR RUBY
THE STUFFED BEAR MYSTERY
THE MYSTERY OF ALLIGATOR SWAMP
THE MYSTERY AT SKELETON POINT
THE TATTLETALE MYSTERY
THE COMIC BOOK MYSTERY
THE GREAT SHARK MYSTERY
THE ICE CREAM MYSTERY
THE MIDNIGHT MYSTERY
THE MYSTERY IN THE FORTUNE COOKIE
THE BLACK WIDOW SPIDER MYSTERY
THE RADIO MYSTERY
THE MYSTERY OF THE RUNAWAY GHOST
THE FINDERS KEEPERS MYSTERY
THE MYSTERY OF THE HAUNTED BOXCAR
THE CLUE IN THE CORN MAZE
THE GHOST OF THE CHATTERING BONES
THE SWORD OF THE SILVER KNIGHT
THE GAME STORE MYSTERY
THE MYSTERY OF THE ORPHAN TRAIN
THE VANISHING PASSENGER
THE GIANT YO-YO MYSTERY
THE CREATURE IN OGOPOGO LAKE
THE ROCK 'N' ROLL MYSTERY
THE SECRET OF THE MASK
THE SEATTLE PUZZLE
THE GHOST IN THE FIRST ROW
THE BOX THAT WATCH FOUND
A HORSE NAMED DRAGON
THE GREAT DETECTIVE RACE
THE GHOST AT THE DRIVE-IN MOVIE
THE MYSTERY OF THE TRAVELING TOMATOES

THE SPY GAME
THE DOG-GONE MYSTERY
THE VAMPIRE MYSTERY
SUPERSTAR WATCH
THE SPY IN THE BLEACHERS
THE AMAZING MYSTERY SHOW
THE PUMPKIN HEAD MYSTERY
THE CUPCAKE CAPER
THE CLUE IN THE RECYCLING BIN
MONKEY TROUBLE
THE ZOMBIE PROJECT
THE GREAT TURKEY HEIST
THE GARDEN THIEF
THE BOARDWALK MYSTERY
THE MYSTERY OF THE FALLEN TREASURE
THE RETURN OF THE GRAVEYARD GHOST
THE MYSTERY OF THE STOLEN SNOWBOARD
THE MYSTERY OF THE WILD WEST BANDIT
THE MYSTERY OF THE SOCCER SNITCH
THE MYSTERY OF THE GRINNING GARGOYLE
THE MYSTERY OF THE MISSING POP IDOL
THE MYSTERY OF THE STOLEN DINOSAUR BONES
THE MYSTERY AT THE CALGARY STAMPEDE
THE SLEEPY HOLLOW MYSTERY
THE LEGEND OF THE IRISH CASTLE
THE CELEBRITY CAT CAPER
HIDDEN IN THE HAUNTED SCHOOL
THE ELECTION DAY DILEMMA
THE DOUGHNUT WHODUNIT
THE ROBOT RANSOM
THE LEGEND OF THE HOWLING WEREWOLF
THE DAY OF THE DEAD MYSTERY
THE HUNDRED-YEAR MYSTERY
THE SEA TURTLE MYSTERY
SECRET ON THE THIRTEENTH FLOOR
THE POWER DOWN MYSTERY
MYSTERY AT CAMP SURVIVAL
THE MYSTERY OF THE FORGOTTEN FAMILY
THE SKELETON KEY MYSTERY
SCIENCE FAIR SABOTAGE
THE GREAT GREENFIELD BAKE-OFF
THE BEEKEEPER MYSTERY
NEW! MYSTERY IN THE MAGIC SHOP

GERTRUDE CHANDLER WARNER discovered when she was teaching that many readers who like an exciting story could find no books that were both easy and fun to read. She decided to try to meet this need, and her first book, *The Boxcar Children*, quickly proved she had succeeded.

Miss Warner drew on her own experiences to write the mystery. As a child she spent hours watching trains go by on the tracks opposite her family home. She often dreamed about what it would be like to set up housekeeping in a caboose or freight car—the situation the Alden children find themselves in.

While the mystery element is central to each of Miss Warner's books, she never thought of them as strictly juvenile mysteries. She liked to stress the Aldens' independence and resourcefulness and their solid New England devotion to using up and making do. The Aldens go about most of their adventures with as little adult supervision as possible—something else that delights young readers.

Miss Warner lived in Putnam, Connecticut, until her death in 1979. During her lifetime, she received hundreds of letters from girls and boys telling her how much they liked her books.